DREAM SONG

Sunlight, Moonlight,
Twilight, starlight —
Gloaming at the close of day,
And an owl calling,
Cool dews falling
In a wood of oak and may.

Lantern-light, taperlight,
Torchlight, no-light:
Darkness at the shut of day,
And lions roaring,
Their wrath pouring
In wild waste places far away.

Elf-light, bat-light;
Touchwood-light and toad-light,
And the sea a shimmering gloom of grey,
And a small face smiling
In a dream's beguiling
In a world of wonders far away.

WALTER DE LA MARE

Acknowledgment: The Literary Trustees of Walter de la Mare
and the Society of Authors as their representative.

The Woodcutter's Tale

An illustrated Faery Story

CAROL FLORENCE ✦ EMILY FORD

Ragged Bears

Far, far away there is a hillside — a hillside wearing a winter-dark skirt of trees that reaches down to the river below.

Nestled on the edge of the woods there is a cottage. It's a small cottage, with thick stone walls and a grey slate roof. At dusk, wisps of smoke furl and whirl from out of the chimney. Up, up, up into the air they go and then are gone.

Inside the cottage the floor is scrubbed and swept.
There is a simple wooden table and four chairs.
At mealtimes the fire burns brightly, a big pot
bubbles and boils, and the kettle sings.

This is the home of the Woodcutter and his family.
The Woodcutter worked long and hard gathering wood
from the forest. Each and every day he put on his jacket
and pulled on his boots, and made his way out into the
grey light of morning. He returned only when the day
was dwindling, and night had all but settled in.

He was a gentle man with gentle ways. He never earned more than a few pennies but it didn't much matter to the Woodcutter and his family. Their lives were bound together by love, and a strong belief in counting not coins or notes but their everyday blessings instead. The family ate their supper by candle-light and to them the bowl of stew and hunk of bread was a feast worthy of kings and queens.

When the meal was finished, and all the jobs were done, the children scrambled up the ladder into the sleeping-loft. Up there, at bedtime, their father told them stories from times long ago and places far away — tales of magic and tales of wonder. Stories of adventures with pirates on the high seas, and of encounters with lions on the hot, dry plains. As he spoke he wove a story spell, casting it in and around the children as they settled down under the blankets.

Later, when all the scrabblings and scratchings, the snufflings and snorings had died down, the cottage and its inhabitants slowly sank into a deep, deep sleep.

One night, the Woodcutter had a dream, and in this dream he found himself high up the steep-sided valley, high up above the cottage and the oak forest he knew so well. He was walking on the wide open Common and eventually came across a grove of ancient thorn trees. Strange, wizened trees they were – stark against a wintry sky, with black, brittle limbs low to the ground, bent and twisted.

In his dream, the Woodcutter moved quietly through the grove, drawn towards one of the trees in particular. He stopped in front of it and caught a glimpse of something light and beautiful.

There before him was a Faery sitting
on a branch. She was sitting waiting
– waiting for him! She smiled, and the
Woodcutter's heart was filled with joy.

Then she was gone.

The next day the Woodcutter put on his jacket and pulled on his boots and went out into the forest as he always did.

Today, though,
was different.
He carried the memory
of the dream with him
and his heart stirred. In the
afternoon, when the work was
finished, he picked up his bundle of
wood and walked along the forest path.
But instead of heading for home, he took the
track up the hill past the church, beyond the high
pastures and up out onto the Common, where a
special stillness filled the air.

He walked over the rough grass, and eventually came to a grove of thorns. The Woodcutter stepped into the ring and as he looked around he saw the very tree that had appeared in the dream. Walking towards it, he reached out to touch the wiry trunk and ran his hand along the black branches.

Then he sat down close by the roots. After a while, the Woodcutter stood up and set off for home, turning just for a moment to look at the tree before he left.

Life went on. The days stepped through the year with an ever-lengthening stride.

The first signs of spring began to show themselves with shoots pushing up through the earth.

Buds could be seen on the bushes and birds returned to the hedgerows, filling the air with their song.

The Woodcutter visited the
tree many times. He never
saw the Faery again but he
felt her presence. Often
there was a shimmer of
light, a sparkle on the
tips of the branches, a
hint of laughter on the
breeze. He began to bring little
gifts for her — treasures
from the forest, which he
left tied to the tree with
brightly-coloured ribbons.
He talked to her, telling her of
his loves and his losses — sharing the
story of his life.

—

He poured out his heart
to her and she heard him.
And she loved him.

One day the Faery decided to leave the Woodcutter
a gift in return for those he had left for her.

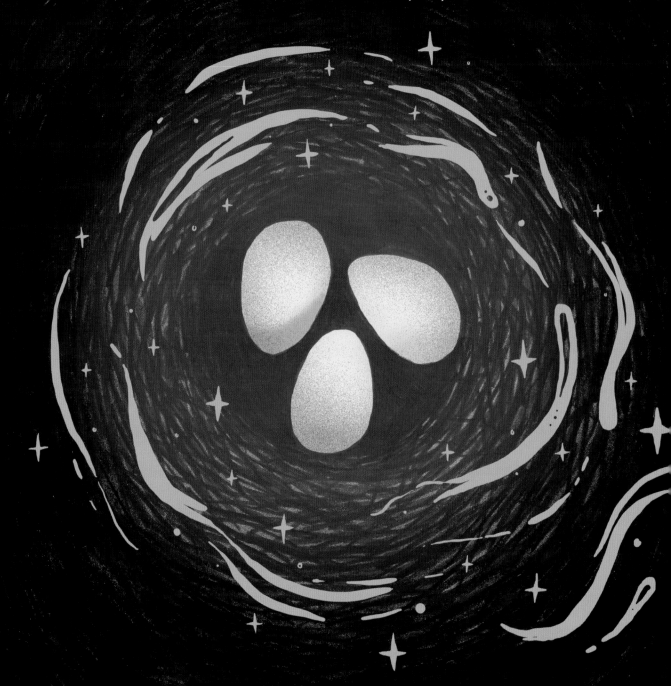

So when he next came to the tree he found a nest
cradled in the roots. Hidden in the nest were three
little eggs — three little eggs made of solid gold.

One by one the Woodcutter carefully lifted
them out and looked at them as they glowed
softly in his hand. He could
hardly believe his eyes.
With his heart pounding,
he set off for home
– the eggs resting
in the nest, and
the nest in
his hands.

He was a gentle man with gentle ways. The last thing he
ever expected was to have been given such a precious gift,
and so it was also beyond him to understand or question
the things that happened on the way back home.

Down he came from the Common; down past the church and down onto the path through the forest.

As his eyes adjusted to the gloom he had a sense that something was coming towards him from out of the shadows.

Suddenly a big black-hooded bird swooped at him, seized one of the eggs, and then was gone! The Woodcutter was stunned, but he steadied himself and carried on. There were still two eggs, and two were plenty.

He was nearly home when he stopped to catch his breath and take a drink from the stream. Kneeling down he placed the nest carefully by his side, and as he drank it began to rock.

The Woodcutter stared in amazement. One of the eggs rolled out into the water, and was gone! Again he was quiet for a moment, but then carried on along the path.

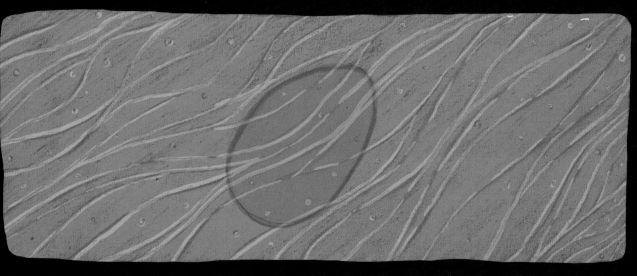

There was still one egg, and that was plenty for him and his family.

Holding the nest close, he arrived home and everyone gathered around the table. When the children and their mother saw the remaining golden egg there were shouts of joy and the house was filled with laughter.

Now, it happened that at that very moment a Drifter was passing by their cottage. The Drifter heard the merriment and sidled up to the window to see what it was all about. He scowled when he saw the dancing and the smiles on their faces. He watched closely as the Woodcutter placed the egg in a jar high up on a shelf. Later that night, when the family were sleeping, the Drifter crept in and stole the egg and all their dreams for the future.

The next morning the Woodcutter put on his jacket and pulled on his boots to go out into the forest as he always did. Just before leaving the house he reached up for the jar to look at the egg. Of course, it had gone! He stepped out into the grey light of morning, and this gentle man with gentle ways didn't know what to think or to do. He felt so foolish for having lost not one, not even two but three precious gifts.

That day he worked slowly and carefully but with a heavy heart. As he worked, he reminded himself that his life, and that of his family, was still held together by kindness and by the grace of their everyday blessings.

At the end of the day the Woodcutter set off for home. When he was walking along the path he noticed the glow of blossom in the hedge and reached up to pick a small

sprig. As he did so, his hand came onto something round — something shaped like a nest. He felt along the edges and then gently inside. There in the middle was an egg. He lifted it out very carefully and looked at it. It was a golden egg!

He rushed home and as he came towards the cottage his wife ran out to meet him. She was smiling as she reached out her hand, and in her outstretched palm was another golden egg! Their son, she said, had caught a fine fish for supper. They had cleaned it and in its belly was the egg.

That night the family celebrated, and that night the Drifter passed by their home again and heard their singing and the merry music.

He was confused. Hadn't he stolen the golden egg? Hadn't he stolen their dreams? He peered in through the window and saw the two eggs glistening and glimmering on the table. He saw the family's joy and delight and his stony heart melted.

Later, when all were sleeping, the Drifter crept into the house and returned the third egg to the jar, and then he left.

The cottage
and its inhabitants

And now, as our story draws to a close, we leave the small
cottage nestled on the edge of the woods, with its thick
stone walls and its grey slate roof. We watch as the wisps
of smoke furl and whirl from out of the chimney. Up, up,
up into the air they go, and then are gone.

The family sit down and have supper together, and then at bedtime the children scramble up the ladder into the sleeping-loft where they hear stories from long ago and far away. Let's leave them now as they all drift off to sleep. Let's leave them to live their lives in peace, and in plenty, with the presence of the Faery always in their hearts.

THE END

For M, L and H
– with love
CAROL FLORENCE

The themes of receiving, losing, and then
re-finding magical gifts occur in tales from many
cultures. I first came across a version of this
story in Storymaking in Education and Therapy
by Alida Gersie and Nancy King.

First published in 2019 by Ragged Bears Ltd
Sherborne, DT9 3PH
www.ragged-bears.co.uk

ISBN: 9781857144796

Text copyright © Carol Florence 2019
Illustrations © Emily Ford 2019
Moral rights asserted

001

A CIP catalogue record for this book is available from the British Library